WAY

P9-EEN-858

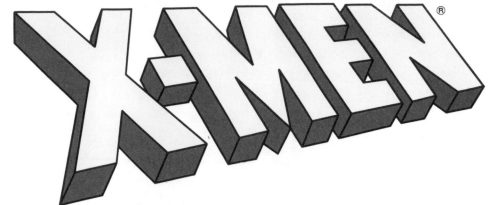

# NIGHT OF THE SENTINELS

**based on a teleplay by Mark Edward Edens**
**illustrated by Marie Severin**
**cover painting by The Thompson Brothers**

NOTE TO READER: Definitions for underlined words can be found in the glossary at the back of the book.

Random House New York

Copyright © 1993 by Marvel Entertainment Group, Inc. All rights reserved under International and Pan-American Copyright Conventions.
Published in the United States by Random House, Inc., New York, and simultaneously in Canada by Random House of Canada Limited, Toronto.
Library of Congress Catalog Card Number: 93-86034  ISBN: 0-679-85708-7
Manufactured in the United States of America  10 9 8 7 6 5 4

Meanwhile, the X-Men's Blackbird jet returned home to the X-Mansion, site of Professor Xavier's School for Gifted Youngsters and training ground for the young mutant X-Men. There the X-Men learned that their colleague Morph was dead, and that fellow mutant Beast had been arrested for <u>subversion</u> and was in jail awaiting trial!

I KNOW YOU FEEL BADLY.

YOU DON'T KNOW NOTHIN', LITTLE MAN.

Wolverine stormed out…he didn't need to listen to the feeble <u>condolences</u> of that goody-goody Cyclops. He needed to be alone with his pain.

Back at the mansion, while watching the President on TV, Cyclops hatched a plan.

That evening, the President sent for Gyrich and told him to shut down the <u>Mutant Registration Program</u>. Gyrich hid his anger.

THOSE MUTANTS WERE WILLING TO SACRIFICE THEIR LIVES. DID THEY HAVE *GOOD* REASON TO FEEL THREATENED?

BRRING!

Just outside the President's office, Gyrich's portable phone rang.

It was Jubilee's father. Cyclops was at his house!

ONE OF THE MUTANTS IS HERE!

KEEP HIM THERE!

Gyrich sent a <u>Sentinel</u> to capture the mutant.

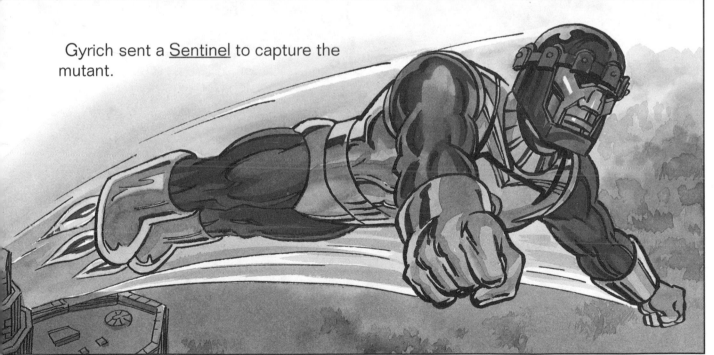

The Sentinel's arm crashed onto a neighbor's lawn!

The Blackbird took off in pursuit of the wounded Sentinel. Cyclops' plan was working like a charm!

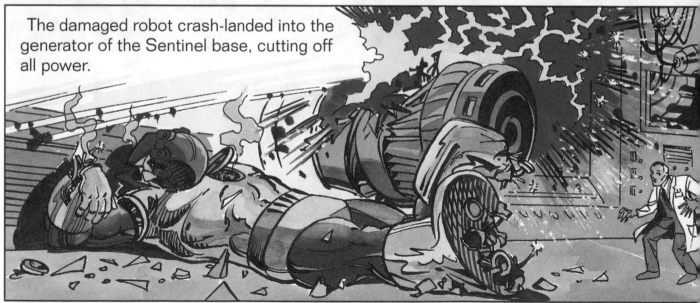

The damaged robot crash-landed into the generator of the Sentinel base, cutting off all power.

Jubilee's <u>electromagnetic</u> cuffs suddenly came loose! She sat up and grinned.

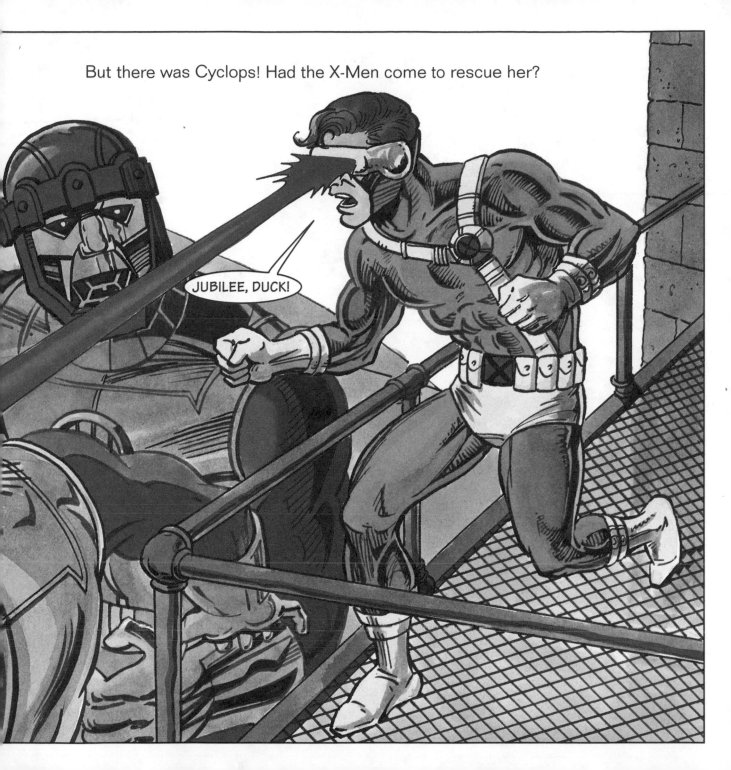

Storm lured one Sentinel high up into the clouds…

…then zapped him back to earth with a lightning bolt!

Another Sentinel pounded Rogue into the floor. She shook her head and got up...

Y'ALL OUGHTA LEARN HOW TO BEHAVE!

...and promptly hammered that robot into scrap metal!

Wolverine leaped onto the back of the last Sentinel…and clawed his way upward until he reached its neck. With a mighty cry, he plunged his <u>adamantium claws</u> into its neck!

CHUCK!

It was time for Jubilee to say good-bye to her foster parents. She knew now that Professor X's School for Gifted Youngsters was the best place for her. There, she would take her rightful place with the other X-Men, and learn how to use her mutant powers for the benefit of mankind.

# GLOSSARY

**adamantium claws:** Wolverine's claws and skeleton are bonded with adamantium, the hardest known metal in the Marvel Universe. The claws can cut through anything—except more adamantium.

**condolences:** Expressions of sympathy to a person who is feeling sadness or grief.

**electromagnetism:** Magnetic energy produced by electric current.

**mutant:** A person born with abilities far beyond those of ordinary humans. A mutant can look like an average human being or not, depending on the particular mutation. Many people are afraid of mutants and their powers.

**Mutant Control Agency:** A government organization set up to find mutants, keep track of them, and capture them if they harm anyone. It is run by Henry Peter Gyrich, who hates mutants and thinks they should all be in prison.

**mutant registration files:** The Mutant Control Agency keeps a file, including the mutant's real name, address, powers, and appearance, on every mutant it finds. When it wants to apprehend a mutant, it can use the file to locate him or her.

**Mutant Registration Program:** A government project aimed at finding mutants who are in hiding and forcing them to register themselves with the Mutant Control Agency.

**Sentinels:** Giant robots created by the Mutant Control Agency to hunt and catch mutants.

**subversion:** Crimes against the government.

**X-Men:** A group of mutants brought together by Professor Charles Xavier. Their goal is to protect both humans and mutants from those mutants who would do them harm. They seek to promote peaceful coexistence between humans and mutants. They are sworn to protect a world that often fears and hates them. Led by Storm and Cyclops, the current membership includes Wolverine, Beast, Jubilee, Rogue, Gambit, and Jean Grey.